E
RA

Radlauer, Ruth

Molly at the
library

W9-CIA-844

$8.95

DATE			
JY 07 '88	JY 27 '89	JA 24 '91	JY 12 '99
AG 5 '88	AG 2 '89	JY 29 '91	JE 19 '92
OC 27 '88	OC 28 '89		JE 28 '93
DE 13 '88	JY 10 '90	AG 28 '91	JUN 8 '94
FE 16 '89	JY 12 '90	SE 19 '91	MAR 21 '98
MR 4 '89	OC 22 '90	SF 19 '91	OCT 17 '95
MR 24 '89	NO 15 '90	NO 7 '91	NOV 04 '95
AP 28 '89	NO 22 '90	DE 6 '91	JUN 19 '98
JE 28 '89		MR 30 '92	JUN 28 '98
			AP 07 '01
			JY 21 '01
			AG 04 '03
			AG 15 '03
			AG 24 '05
			MR 27 '06

Molly at the Library

by Ruth Shaw Radlauer

illustrated by Emily Arnold McCully

Simon & Schuster Books for Young Readers
Published by Simon & Schuster Inc., New York

Published by Simon & Schuster Books for Young Readers
A Division of Simon & Schuster Inc.
Simon & Schuster Building, Rockefeller Center
1230 Avenue of the Americas, New York, NY 10020

10   9   8   7   6   5   4   3   2   1

Simon & Schuster Books for Young Readers
is a trademark of Simon & Schuster, Inc.
Printed in Spain

Library of Congress Cataloging in Publication Data
Radlauer, Ruth, 1926-
Molly at the library.
Summary: Four-year-old Molly goes to the library
with her father and is thrilled to discover that she
can take home ten books for fourteen days.
[1. Libraries—Fiction.   2. Reading—Fiction]
I. McCully, Emily Arnold, ill.   II. Title.
PZ7.R122Mnt   1987   [E]   87-14385
ISBN 0-671-66166-3

To my indispensable friends,
the librarians

Molly went to the library with her

She went to the children's room.
"Look at all those books," Molly said
in her outdoors voice.
Everyone looked at her.

Then Molly remembered to use
her secret-telling voice.
"I like this book about lizards,"
she said.

"Oh, I love birds.
I want this book.

"I want this book,
   and this other book too."

"Molly," said the librarian,
"you may check out ten books
for two weeks."

Molly took ten books home.
Dad read to her every day
for two weeks.

Mom read to Molly every night
for two weeks.

After two weeks, Molly and her dad
went to the library again.
Molly turned her books in
at the desk.

Then she went
to the children's room.

In her secret-telling voice, Molly said,
"I can check out ten more books."
She found one about boats
and one about snakes.
That was two.

"Here's one about dogs," Molly said.
"That's three.
And Goldilocks makes four.
Tractors—that's five.

"This story about a kitten makes six.
Snails—seven.
Shells—eight.
This one about a queen makes nine,
and one more about trees is ten."

Molly took home ten new books.
"Look, Mom," Molly said.
"What a lot of books to read,"
said Mom.

"Every night," said Molly.
"And every day," said Mom.

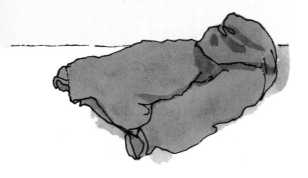

"All ten of them every night
and every day," Molly said.
"Let's start right now!"